THIS BOOK
BELONGS TO:

_____

DATE RECEIVED: _____

Deep in the ocean, in the coral reef, among the shipwrecks and seaweed, the ocean creatures live and play. Here is what happened to them one fine day.

On their way to school, Manny the Mandarinfish, Seth the Seahorse, and Abby the Angelfish decided they would race to see who would get there the fastest.

Manny took the lead early.
The group zoomed through
seaweed and zipped through
coral. Seth and Abby
continued to fall behind
as the race went on.

After a while, Seth and Abby could no longer see Manny. Suddenly, they both noticed that there was something in the water up ahead.

"Is that Walter Whale?"
asked Abby.

"I'm not sure," replied Seth.
"He's not moving; I wonder if
he's alright. We should go
check on him."

"What about Manny,"
asked Abby.

"He'll be okay," said Seth,
"We're so far behind, he won't
even notice."

Meanwhile, Manny made it to school in record time. "I win!" he exclaimed. As Manny turned around, he noticed that Seth and Abby were missing.

"Abby? Seth? Where are you guys?" called Manny. There was no response. "I didn't realize I was that fast," he said to himself.

Manny waited and waited. Still there was no Abby and no Seth.

"I wonder where they could be," he thought. "Something's fishy here. I'd better go look for them," he decided.

Manny retraced the path
he took on the way to the
school. He looked everywhere
he could think of, still Manny
found no trace of Seth or
Abby.

Manny was about halfway back to where they had started the race when he heard voices coming from behind him.

"Is it him?" asked one of the voices.

"I still can't tell," said the other voice.

When Manny finally discovered where the voices were coming from, he was surprised to see Seth and Abby casually swimming away from the school.

"There you are!" called Manny, "I've been looking everywhere for you guys! Where have you been?"

"We think we can see Walter and he looks sick. Could you come and help?" replied Seth.